A DAY BETWEEN JOY RD AND CHICAGO

Told by Paul B McCallum

*I dedicate this, my first book, to my wife
Erika who has supported me throughout
all my journeys and my cousin (more like
brother) Shawn, who showed me the way and
gave me the inspiration for this story.*

CONTENTS

MOSES

"How did I get here again? Where did Davion go? And who put this blunt in my hand?" The young man said to a response of resounding laughter from the congregation of the drunk and disorderly... except for one solitary and assertive tone of disgust and condemnation.

"Yall know that boy don't do no real drugs!" Sarge exclaims.

Moses goes over the information rapidly escaping his short-term memory. "Me and Davion smoked a blunt from his crib and made me hang out with these bums. That's Sarge, I guess he would be considered their leader. He's a war vet. Which war? I don't even think he knows. The greasy mouthed guy is Catfish, because he always looks and smells like he's been eating fish. The dirty pimp with the Borsalino, and chipped cane is Stack-a-Dollars, even though he looks like a pocket-o-change. The raspy voice older guy is Candyman. He used to have the sweetest singing voice until he got shot in the neck. The big snaggled tooth, midnight train to Harlem, is Baghdad the bum formerly known as sasquatch." His mind is racing and is only getting as far as the group around him before he cycles back to his original thought, except this time all rational versions are gone.

"How did I get here again? And who put this blunt in my hand?" Holy shit I'm freaking out.

"Yall know that boy don't do no real drugs!" I hear the army nigga say.

"We don't know shit until somebody tell us shit. That ain't my son." The big hairy one says, still laughing with the rest of these old heads. Let me think. I remember talking to some dude about smoking some weed and then meeting up with these dudes about some ...church shit.

"Nephew! Are you alright?" The one with the fish face is talking to me. Why the fuck do his skin got scales on it!?

"Yeah, fish nigga." I need to let this fishy ass dude know he can't scare me. Let me stand up so he can see my feet. "Are YOU alright!?"

"It's cool nephew, he didn't know you didn't know. Just sit back down and let me get that out your hand." When did this army nigga put on a uniform and where did he get that helmet? He must be for real.

"Sir, yes sir!" That should let him know I'm a good

soldier.

"Good job Sarge but I bet you couldn't get him to march in the store and get this drank." Now the one with money falling out his mouth wants me to go buy him a drank. Something ain't right. I can't remember my mission. I need my weapon.

"Fuck this shit! I thought you were a colonel 'Sarge'? You wierdo mutherfuckas can't trick me with all this Halloween make up." They don't know that I keep one in the chamber. The first one of these mutants move is gonna catch it.

"Nephew relax, we don't want no trouble. We just trying to get high and talk some shit." Is this furball trying to grab me with his arms up like that? "Come on man, I thought you said you wanted to throw some bones or something." Bones? Is he trying to eat me?

"Yeah, let's just shoot some crap nephew please." Sarge is right.

"By your command!" First shot right in big foots head. I don't know why they're running. Fish face can't swim on land. I need to put him out of his misery next. I let those two shots off too fast. He is flopping on the ground like I missed once.

"NEPHEW, CHILL THE FUCK OUT! This is ain't you. It's that shit in the blunt. PLEASE STOP SHOOTING!" I get it now. Sarge and his crew is trying to poison me. I won't fall for his shit again.

"I'll stop shooting when all y'all crazy muthafuckas are dead." I love the sound the draco makes when I shoot at hoe ass niggas trying to play me. Sarge can move for an old head. He got behind that dumpster real quick. I can handle him last. I gotta get that money talking ass nigga before he get in the gas station across the street. He can't outrun these bullets but he running straight for the pack of fine bitches. "Stop running before I hit somebody by mistake."

"I'M SORRY NEPHEW! PLEASE DON'T KILL ME! PLE..." Got his ass but the fish nigga is still rolling on the ground. I really need to work on my aim.

"Can you hear me fish nigga? Say sorry." I need to shoot him again because I don't think he heard me. "I said, CAN YOU HEAR ME?" I guess not. Maybe, I shouldn't have shot him in the head first.

 "Is he ok, girl?" Look at that ass and so sweet trying to save that loser. She doesn't know that he is crazy and might try to poison her too. I need to end this now.

"Sarge, wait there. I have to cancel that money talking fool before he fucks it up with my new baby mama." Let me take my time walking over there. I don't want her to think I'm too anxious.

"What's up ladies? No need to panic. I'm going to take care of this piece of shit before he poison y'all too." I see one of them has their phone out. "Get this right here sweetheart. I'm about to make ou r community safe again." Let me focus my attention on this evil creature threatening my neighborhood and future wife.

"No amount of crawling is going to save you. Get your hand off that door. Those Arabs don't want you dying in their gas station."

"Fuck you, I already told you I'm sorry and you still just gonna shoot me for nothing. Get this shit over with."

"No problem, it would be my pleasure." I hope she can see how cool and smooth I am when killing niggas. Now all I need to do is go finish up with Sarge and get back to wifey and her bad ass friends.

"Run you crazy ass nigga! The police are coming!" I knew she liked me. Look at her all concerned for my safety.

"Don't worry my beautiful queen. This will only take a minute. Sarge, don't move I'm on my way." Luckily, I can still see his shadow behind the dumpster. "I promise it will be over quick." I need to make sure my future baby mama knows that she is my number 1 priority after this is over. "My apologies, but I didn't introduce myself. They call me Moses."

"Get the fuck away from us you psycho!" I don't care about this one talking she is not as thick as my boo.

"Shut up bitch!"

"Who he calling a bitch?!" This skinny bitch just

maced me. I can't believe it.

"Bitch I'm trying to save your stupid ass and this is how you do me." My eyes are on fire. "What the fuck is in that shit?" What the fuck is that sound? "Who tripped me?" I think that sounds like bus brakes.

"Watch out!" Is this the last thing that I hear. Nope. It's definitely the bus brakes.

BLACK GIRL MAGIC

"Nadia, hurry up! HE IS NOT THERE! Let's go, damn!" Robin says from the front seat of the car out the open passenger door to an irate Nadia pounding on the front door of Davion's house.

"Davion open the fucking door! I see your car, stupid ass nigga! I know you in there with some bitch. Fuck you! You can't do me like this!" Nadia spits on the window and starts walking towards the car. "Fuck him! Let's get up outta here before I do something crazy." She turns around and throws the bottle of cognac she's holding on the porch.

"Why do we always have to go through this shit with her and Davion?" Robin says to Stephanie when she sees Nadia throw the bottle. "This bitch is tripping for real." She starts blowing the horn then Stephanie drops the weed out of the blunt she's rolling.

"What the fuck Robin! You just made me spill the weed all over myself blowing the horn like that." She starts brushing the crumbs on the floor when Nadia finally makes it back to the car, still upset and slams the door.

"Let's go! He ain't shit!" Nadia says fighting the angry tears and still holding on to the door handle.

"Yall bitches are really effin' up my day. First you throw the Remy I BOUGHT on the porch, then this heffer in the backseat waste MY WEED and then proceeds to brush that shit on the floor and then you get your heavy-handed self in the car and slam my mothafuckin door. I know it's about you right now and what you're going through but that don't mean you're going to be treating me like I ain't shit. That nigga Davion aint shit! Oh, and did I mention, Stephanie just wasted the last blunt."

Nadia switches back to her confident yet sweet tone without shedding the tear she was fighting. "I'm sorry girl. You know I can overreact when it comes to my heart and I'm so glad y'all always got my back."

"I'm sorry too." Stephanie chimes in. "You know I get jumpy around loud noises."

"We good but we are not about to hug it out. If I didn't have to pee, I could think of more shit to say besides I love y'all too and Stephanie wasted the last blunt."

"You must be big mad. Next round is on me and I will vacuum the backseat." Stephanie says looking through her purse.

"Girl, quit playing. I told you that everything is on me and I don't have time to wait while you look for your black card that's in 'my other purse'. I still gotta pee." Robin says as she pulls off towards the liquor store/gas station/weed spot/day club on Joy Rd.

"Bitch please. I'm not worried about you. I'm looking for my lip gloss since I'm not rolling up again."

"You didn't roll up the first time, Miss 'I hate loud noises.'" Robin starts to speed up as she begins to squirm in the seat. "I really need to pee so let's focus on that."

"If you have to pee so bad then why don't you whip your dick out and piss in that cup since she-hulk smashed the bottle of Remy." Stephanie says while holding a red solo cup and smirking at Robin.

"Bitch cause I'm a real lady with dignity and I'm not going to piss in a fucking cup in a car. Plus, I hate looking at soft dicks and only a real woman can appreciate that and know my true suffering. Long story short. I'm about to pull in this alley, squat, piss, and wipe while you look out and get ready to go in the store and find a nigga to roll up if not buy the weed. So keep getting pretty, because I stay pretty." She adjusts her breasts with one hand while blowing kisses in the rearview mirror.

"Whatever, you just mad your eyes ain't as pretty as mine."

"Alright, alright. We get it. We all some bad bitches and hard dicks are the only dicks that matter.

Pussies like Davion deserved to get fucked." Nakia exclaims right before applying her lip gloss in the mirror and to the sigh of Stephanie and Robin. "We're about to go do just like Robin said and go finesse a good time for the sake of the sisterhood."

"Amen. Now watch the alley while I do my thang." Robin hops out the car after finally making it to the security of the familiar neighborhood alleyway and the others finish prettying up before heading to the front of the store to complete the mission of celebrating the liberation of Nadia of her abusive drug dealer boyfriend.

After the buzz from a refill of drinks and "donations" from thirsty prey falling into their trap kicks in, Robin notices Moses walking across the street towards the church and tries to catch his eye but he doesn't notice her. Maintaining her ladylike status refuses to get his direct attention and decides that she needs another opportunity to lure him in indiscreetly discrete. "Did y'all see that fine ass nigga across the street?"

"Who? The tall nigga with the bums at the church? He cute but, DAMN, he hanging with the crackhead drunks at the church." Nadia retorts with disdain and a hint of disappointment.

"He is too clean to be a bum and I just heard one of 'em say 'nephew' so you know he got love for his people. Don't act like you don't have a drunk uncle or two or three. Besides, I just get that vibe from him. I like the way he moves." Robin licks her lips and then bites the bottom one. "Mm. Mm. Mmm."

Nadia and Stephanie look at each other and burst out laughing. Nadia stops laughing long enough to blurt out, "This bitch then fell in love with the way a nigga walks!"

Stephanie still chuckling, "That's what we get for switching to tequila. She always get extra **extra** with that silver."

"We are wasting time. My boo can't see my ass from here. Let's walk around to the gas station and get another bag so he can get a better look." She says while semi twerking around the car.

While walking towards the gas station, all three are laughing, giggling, or smiling for their respective reasons, when they hear the first shots. "I think your nigga is a little violent Robin." Stephanie says while ducking behind Nadia.

"I know right. He is a warrior and I'm his Wakandan princess. Matter of fact I need to get this on my live." Robin reaches for her phone and starts her livestream.

Nadia is captivated by the ruckus and gets out her phone too. "I finally get a WorldStar moment on camera."

Stephanie amazed by her friends' courage under fire asks, "Why are we still here like those aint real bullets? Yall acting like Live and WorldStar pay the bills."

"Onlyfans pays the bills. My Live, Instagram, and TikTok, is advertising boo boo, Okay. Secondly, nobody is shooting at us or in our direction so just relax and take notes from a real stallion" Robin does her Live intro and then pauses the recording. "As a matter of fact. Why don't you hold Nadia's phone while me and Nadia hold the sisterhood down." Nadia hands her phone to Stephanie and gets close to Robin to be included in the selfie intro. "I'm with my homegirls Nasty_Nadia and That_Girl_Steph and it's the one and only Robin_The_Realest...*trademark coming...*We out here on the streets of Detroit. Some of y'all might say 'Dietroit' and today I am bearing witness to niggas getting shot at a church." She stops before she can say another word when Moses finally makes eye contact with her before he chases one of the bums across the street to the gas station. Robin tries to stop the bum before he has a chance to bleed on her shoes.

"Is he ok, girl?" Stephanie asks Robin as she guides him toward the gas station.

"Hell naw, don't you see all this blood." She helps him stay on his feet then gently pushes him towards the gas station door when she sees Moses approaching.

"What's up ladies? No need to panic. I'm going to take care of this piece of shit before he poisons y'all too." He notices the phone in Stephanie's hand. "Get this right here sweetheart. I'm about to make our community safe again." He continues the chase trying to be Idris Elba smooth while murdering the unfortunate soul who started his day just trying to escape sobriety. Robin notices the flirting the moment he made eye contact with her when he said, "No problem, it would be my pleasure." And proceeded to kill the poor drunk in cold blood.

Robin snaps back to reality due to the point-blank shooting. "Run you crazy ass nigga! The police are coming!"

"Don't worry my beautiful queen. This will only take a minute." He turns and yells to the last vagrant standing (hiding behind a dumpster), "Sarge, don't move I'm on my way. I promise it will be over quick." He returns his attention to Robin and in his smoothest deepest voice he admits, "My apologies, but I didn't introduce myself. They call me Moses."

"Get the fuck away from us you psycho!" Nadia shouts while stepping closer to Robin and Moses.

"Shut up bitch!" He yells while turning to face her.

"Who he calling a bitch?!" Stephanie chimes in right before she maces him with the can she's been clutching since Nadia first handed her the phone.

"Bitch I'm trying to save your stupid ass and this is how you do me." He starts gagging, coughing, and stumbling around. "What the fuck is in that shit?"

"Watch out!" Robin screams as he trips, falls in the street and gets run over by the bus. She sees the gun slide right in front of her and she picks it up.

Nadia grabs Stephanie who is screaming and they start running towards the car. "Robin stop trippin' and let's go!" she says while holding back the laughter caused by the scream Stephanie just made. "Look! Even the mailman shaking his head at your silly ass. At least hit the button so we can get into the car. Damn!" she says as she slaps the roof of the car in rhythm with her words.

Robin pauses in her admiration of the new party favor left by her almost dearly yet still departed 'warrior king' and unlocks the car door before gleefully skipping to the car with the gun in one hand and her phone in the other. "Who Live is better than mine?!" she says rotating the phone to show her followers the carnage left in the wake of Moses.

"Bitch stop streaming!" looks at Stephanie "You, stop screaming!" looks back at Robin "Now drive so we can get the fuck out of here before twelve show up while you got the murder weapon in your hand." Nadia calms when Robin and Stephanie comply and starts searching for what's left of the alcohol.

Robin starts to pull out of the parking lot while still recording. "I don't know why you tripping so hard." She says to Nadia before addressing the camera. "She's acting like the police actually do their job, show up on time, or even give a fuck about us or our neighborhood but I'm not going to get my Angela Davis on with a black power speech today. Right now, we just focusing on nigga shit and that's today's hot topic. This is your girl Robin_The_Realest signing off!" She puts the phone down and picks the gun up off her lap and shows it to the other two. "Now what do we do with this?"

Nadia takes a shot and passes the bottle back to Stephanie. "Steph hold this." She notices that Stephanie is still shaken up. "Matter of fact, drink that. A lot." She then grabs the gun from Robin with a devilish grin. "I know exactly what we can do."

"I hope you ain't trying to shoot Davion." Stephanie says while taking another big gulp of alcohol.

"Nope, not shoot him. Shoot AT him maybe. Shoot up his car, good chance. Make him suffer, without a doubt." She says while looking blankly through the window with an even more maniacal grin and a blank stare. "Are y'all down?"

"Whatever makes you happy girl. You know I'm with you but I gotta record some of this for my channel." She tries handing Stephanie the phone. "I mean can you record this for me since I'm driving."

"Ride or die till the day we die." She snatches the phone out of Robin's hands. "Why do we have to always get into loud shit? Yall are so irritating."

The trip to Davion's house was full of excitement and anticipation as they approached the house. Nadia is getting antsy as she notices a girl walking from the back of the house. "I can't believe this nigga got a bitch at his house already."

"Look at her. She is probably still in high school." Stephanie says with a little chuckle. "I didn't know that nigga was a pedophile."

"Well, she is about to learn a valuable lesson today." Nadia opens the door with the pistol in hand.

"Aw shit, come on before she kills that little girl." Stephanie says to Robin who is checking her make up in the rearview mirror.

"She ain't gone shoot her." She pauses for a moment and makes eye contact with Stephanie in the mirror. "Naw, you right. Let's go but keep the camera rolling."

They both jump out the car to intervene but Nadia has already pistol whipped the unsuspecting girl to the ground and is kicking her in the stomach. "Come get your bitch Davion!" she yells towards the house. "I hope you pregnant bitch so I can murder this baby too!" she screams at the girl while continuing to kick her in the stomach. "Come save your bitch, hoe ass nigga." The girl fights back and grabs Nadia's leg causing her to fall. She gets up and tries to run. "Grab the bitch!"

Robin catches her within a couple steps and slams her to the ground. "Got her!" She struggles a bit and the girl is able to get to her knees but Robin still is able to put her in a headlock. "Stephanie make sure you get a good angle on my ass if you not going to help."

"Don't worry about me. Yall are doing a great job without me and I don't need to be playing in the dirt with these nails." She says while capturing the moment and making 'duck lips' towards the camera.

Nadia back to her feet and angrier than before charges at the girl with the gun leading the way directly to her face. "ON GOD! Try that shit again and I will end you right here!"

Stephanie kicks her in the hip causing her to fall completely back to the ground which also causes Robin to let go of her choke hold. "About time but DAMN STEPH! You can warn a bitch before you 'Sparta' kick a hoe." She checks one of her rings, pulls the hair caught in out and shows it to the phone and Stephanie simultaneously. "See. This could have been my hair instead of this trifling hoe's right here."

Nadia grabs the back of the girl's hair and pulls her to her knees. Her hands instinctively go up as her head raises to meet eyes with Nadia. Her voice is remarkably calm despite the adrenaline she's feeling. "My name is N'vaeh. I just came to drop this money off to Davion that my momma owed him."

Nadia pushes hard on the back of N'vaeh's head forcing her to be on all fours. "Run this bitch pockets. See if she got some money." Robin and Stephanie search both sides of her pants since they are standing on opposite sides. Robin pulls out a few hundred dollars cash and Stephanie pulls out a phone. Nadia unphased by the contents of her pockets. "So what bitch. That don't mean shit. He probably just paid your ass for some pussy." She looks at her cohorts and gives them a nod and a grin. "That's y'all shit. Put it away before someone try to rob you." They each look at each other and pause for a moment, then Robin tucks the money in her bra and Stephanie does the same with the phone. Nadia returns her attention to N'vaeh. "Now tell Davion to bring his pedophile tricking ass out here, you lying baby hoe."

"I already told you. I just came here to pay Davion the money that my mother owed him but he is not here. I was just leaving to go home when y'all jumped me. Please give me the money back so I can pay him." She says looking at all three, searching for a bit of sympathy or at least mercy before resting her gaze back at Nadia.

The lack of fear in N'vaeh's eyes only angered Nadia more and she began to drag her by the hair towards the car ensuring that N'vaeh stayed on all fours. "We about to take this bitch for a ride."

"My girls ain't no joke." Stephanie pans around as all four head toward the car and focuses on Nadia passing the gun to Robin to get a better grip on N'vaeh's hair. "She is literally dog walking this bitch by her hair like a leash." She returns focus back to Robin. "And we got The Realest holding it down like the secret service but for real bitches." Robin blows a kiss and strikes a pose. Stephanie looks at Nadia a little confused. "But for real though, where are we going?"

"Like I said 'for a ride'. Get in the car doggy. It's time to go." Nadia says before pushing N'vaeh into the backseat. "Robin gimme something to tie her hands up with."

"Why do you think I got whips and chains....in my car?" Robin says while winking at Stephanie still recording.

"Just give me something. She's a feisty lil bitch." Nadia struggles a bit restraining N'vaeh when she looks down and sees a purse behind the seat. "Stephanie grab that purse and take off the strap so I can tie her hands up. Robin keep the gun in her face until we tie her up. If she even look like she want to fight hit her in those puppy dog eyes." N'vaeh submits and Nadia starts to tie her wrists together.

"You do have some pretty eyes girl. I'm glad you decided to relax because I would hate to mess up the pair." Suddenly Robin's face lights up, looks at the gun, and gasps. "Oh shit! I know where we should go next." She dances with the gun for a moment then sets it on her lap, puts the car in gear and drives off.

"Ok then. So where are we going?" Stephanie says even more puzzled but still laughing.

"We are going to Corey's house to fuck with him now. On god, I've been waiting to get him back."

Robin says with a devilish grin.

"Are you talking about Corey from down the street from your grandma house?"

"Yup. This has been a long time coming."

"You still holding grudges from elementary school." Stephanie laughs hysterically. "He was pretty mean but damn. It's all good girl. We with you."

"Sounds like fun." Nadia says while not breaking eye contact with N'vaeh. "Doesn't it puppy bitch?" N'vaeh's response was only to look at Stephanie.

They take a short ride to Corey's two family flat lightly tormenting N'vaeh in preparation for the confrontation with Robin's childhood bully. Nadia primarily just slapping her in the back of the head pushing her forehead with the sharpest fingernail every time Robin made a point and Stephanie just repeating 'stupid bitch' every couple of seconds. Once they arrive Robin goes over the plan.

"First, we set up in the house. They always leave the side door open. Stephanie, you and Nadia knock on the downstairs door and ask for Jabari. I'll stay on the landing by the back door with the pup out of sight. When he comes to the door flirt with him and convince him to let y'all inside. As soon as y'all walk past him pick something up, twerk, or do something so that he's looking at your ass and then I'm going to bust in and take over. Y'all got it?" Robin looks at the group for understanding.

"What should we say so that he'll let us in?" Stephanie asks with genuine confusion.

"Who cares. Quit acting like you ain't never finessed a nigga. Do the same shit from earlier and just act like you trying to smoke. This nigga ain't going to refuse smoking with two pretty ass bitches." Robin thinks for a second. "Matter of fact, you probably don't have to say anything. Just adjust them titties, get those lips popping, and spray some this on you." She reaches in the glove box and grabs a bottle of Victoria secret body spray.

"Are there any more questions?"

N'vaeh looks up sheepishly. "Can I please just go home?"

"You can leave when the ride is over skanky puppy?" Nadia tells N'vaeh with her first smile since leaving for Corey's house.

"Just be cool and don't do anything stupid and everything will work out nicely." Stephanie says in a calm and soothing tone.

"Yeah. If you don't fuck this up for me, I'll take you home." Robin says almost like a plea. "Right Nadia?"

Nadia hesitantly agrees. "If and only IF she behaves like a good doggie." She snatches N'vaeh by the back the head and leans toward her ear. "Are you going to be a good doggie?" N'vaeh nods in agreement and says yes.

"We ready?" Robin looks at their faces for

acknowledgment. "Alright then. Let's do it. Ride or die..."

Nadia, Stephanie, and Robin in unison. "Until the day we die!"

The plan plays out just as Robin predicted and Corey is on the floor confused by everything happening so fast. "What the fuck is this about?" He says looking down the barrel of the gun that Robin is holding. He tries to stand but Robin cocking the gun makes him stay on his knees. "Ok, ok, ok. Just tell me what y'all want since y'all obviously aint about to give me no pussy and I ain't got no weed."

"Just shut the fuck up and close your eyes before I close them permanently." Robin then glances over to Stephanie. "Get the phone out and get this. Record. Don't go on my live. I'm going to edit it after this."

"This is how we do bullies in the D. Open your mouth nigga." Corey reluctantly opens his mouth a little. "Nigga open wide and let me see the back of your throat."

"Why? What for?"

Robin fires a shot into the floor. "I'm not going to tell you again and keep your fucking eyes closed." Corey squints his eyes closed and opens his mouth wide. "Good. Look at this bitch on his knees with his mouth open just waiting for somebody to put something long and hard in it." She puts the gun to his bottom lip and scrapes his teeth with the gun. "Uh oh. You know better than to use your teeth." She pistol whips him on the side of the head and he almost falls over. "Now try again. Open up wide or I won't miss this time." She inches closer with the gun. "Keep your eyes closed and stick your tongue out." He does as instructed. Robin looks at Stephanie holding the phone. "This stupid ass nigga think I'm about to mouth rape him with the gun. No form of rape is ok even if this bitch deserves it. But he is worth my spit." She inhales a deep and snotty breath while clearing her throat of all mucus and motioning to the others to do the same. She gives the nod and they all spit in his face with Robin's snotty mouthful going directly in his mouth causing him to gag and puke. They laugh and dry heave simultaneously.

"Why? I'm sorry for whatever I did just leave." Corey says as he wipes his mouth with his hand.

"You don't recognize me now." Robin says in disbelief.

"How the fuck could I? You been beating my ass telling me to keep my eyes closed and spitting in my face and shit. I thought y'all was just some high-quality thots." He looks up still squinting when he finally recognizes Robin. "Holy shit!" He chuckles. "Is that 'faggot-ass-Russell' pretending to be a woman still."

Stephanie and Nadia look at each other and shake their heads and brace for Robin's reaction.

Robin slaps Corey in the face with the side of the gun, forcing two teeth to be ejected from his mouth hitting the floor before the rest of his body. "You hoe ass nigga!" She kicks him in the ribs hard enough to make him gasp and spits on him again. "Don't you ever fucking dead name me!"

Corey staggers himself back to the kneeling position slowly, spitting blood and wiping the residue on his clothes just as slowly. "Yeah. I get it now." His head finally lifted high enough for Robin to see the smirk on his bloody toothless face. "I know you liked it."

Robin becomes enraged and starts to beat him in the head with the gun until he falls to the ground. Stephanie and Nadia's cheers and instigation have changed to silence and concern. Robin leans over him and continues to savagely bash his face with the pistol. "Don't! You! Ever! Fucking!" Her tears and the blows start to fall heavier with each word. "Ever! Fucking! Touch! Meee!"

"Please make her stop!" N'vaeh says to Stephanie breaking the look of shock on her face.

"You made your point. I think he gets it." Stephanie pleads.

Nadia manages to get Robin off of him and onto her feet but not before landing a couple more hits to his lifeless body. "You got his ass. Save some of that energy for Davion."

Robin still in a rage and barely being restrained by Nadia easily breaks free and shoots Corey in the groin. "That's how I liked it!" She allows Nadia to console her by giving her the gun.

Nadia takes the gun from Robin and regains control of the situation. She speaks in a calm yet assertive tone "Robin it's time to go right now! Stephanie, please calm the fuck down with the noise phobia shit. Ho-bitch keep staying chill. We have to get the hell up out of here ASAP." Nadia starts pushing everyone out the house after checking the windows for nosy neighbors. "By the time we get out the front door everybody better be real lady like or its real prison like. Now everybody put on your club face and let's figure out what to do next."

The ladies make it out of the house without incident leaving Corey in two pools of blood on the living room floor. Robin hands Nadia the keys to the car. "I cannot drive right now. My hands are shaking too bad." Nadia grabs the keys and Robin gets in the backseat with N'vaeh. After they all get in the car Robin lets out a loud scream startling Stephanie.

"Shit! Shit! Shit!" Nadia pounds on the dashboard. She closes her eyes and chants. "Think your way out of this woman. Think. Think. Think."

"Let's go to LaVar's spot." Stephanie chimes in after calming herself down with slow breaths. "My cousin will look out for us."

"You right. That nigga always stay getting in and out of shit." Nadia throws the car in gear and speeds towards LaVar's house. Nadia looks in the rear view and sees Robin zoned out staring into nothingness. "Hey! The Realest! Snap out of it." She reaches back and snaps her fingers in Robin's face. "Robin your fans need you to get it together." She looks at Stephanie and motions for her to start recording again. "See, Steph already got you loaded up and we need to see you keep the puppy in line before the ride is over. You can't leave the people hanging. So pull your shit together and rectify this situation while looking good doing it. Right my baby?"

The light returns to Robin's eyes. "You're god damn right! Can't no nigga or no bitch stop me from being the queen that I am." She puts on a smile and faces Stephanie holding the phone. "Please forgive me y'all. I had a moment of strength a minute ago and had to deal with my emotions like a woman has to sometime but I'm back with y'all on this crazy ass journey. So, stay tuned." Her smile drops as soon as Stephanie stops recording. "Alright y'all, I'm cool now let's get this day over with as soon as possible. Somebody pass the rest of that drank so I can calm my nerves."

"Me first." Stephanie grabs the bottle a takes a huge gulp before passing it back to Robin. Robin takes a long drink before passing it up front to Nadia.

"I rather hit the blunt but this will do for now." Nadia relents as she continues to speed to their next destination only slowing down enough so that she doesn't spill anything on her shirt. "Here, give this to the puppy. She might be thirsty too."

"No thank you." N'vaeh vehemently denies the offering.

"Bitch. You don't have a choice. You gone learn not to bite the hand that feeds you." Nadia lashes out after the perceived disrespect.

"Just drink it. Pretend it's a birthday shot. I know it's your birthday today. I saw it on your phone." Stephanie holds up N'vaeh's phone. "If not, I can't promise this will end nice for you." N'vaeh nods slightly with her head and submits with her eyes.

"Tilt your head back." Robin grabs the bottle and begins to pour it into N'vaeh's mouth when the car jolts due to the reckless driving of Nadia. "Damn NaNa. You made me spill this shit on my backseat. Drive normal, nobody is chasing us." She finishes pouring the liquor in her mouth. "That wasn't so bad was it."

N'vaeh glares at Nadia then painstakingly swallows the burning liquid. "Not at all. Happy Birthday to me."

They arrive at Lavar's house with everybody less sober than they were ten minutes ago. "Robin you should stay in the car with her since he is still mad at you about not telling him about your past and putting your tongue in his mouth." Stephanie says in a serious tone.

"Whatever. You know he just mad cause he can't have no more of these luscious lips." Robin blows a kiss at Stephanie.

"I'm serious. You need to stay in the car. We need all the help we can get right now and he is all the help we can get."

"No problem. I got u. I will stay my pretty ass here on guard dog duty."

"Come on Stephanie, you know how he is. Let's get in here and figure this shit out." Nadia says before exiting the vehicle with Stephanie close after. "We shouldn't be too long. Just make sure the puppy stays quiet."

Stephanie calls Lavar on his cell phone. "Hey it's me. I'm outside. Come open up the door."

"Alright here I come. Is old girl with you?"

"Who?" Stephanie feigns surprise.

"You got jokes." LaVar not impressed by her acting.

"You mean Robin. Come on now. It's just me and NaNa."

"You should have said that in the first place. I love her little sexy ass." He opens the door finally. "Come on in." They both enter and he gives them both a hug that lingers for more than a few seconds. "What up doe cuzzo?" He looks at Nadia licking his lips. "Wassup Nadia? When you gone stop frontin' and let me give you some of this dick." He grabs his crotch while still looking at her from breast to ass.

Nadia erupts in laughter. "Nigga please. Even if I thought about fucking you, you'd cum in your pants. You can't handle this wet ass pussy in your dreams so your best bet is to keep dreaming."

LaVar unphased. "No worries. Not today then. Hit me up when you ready for this right here." He grabs his crotch again.

Nadia bats her eyes and smiles at him. "4sho. On the 32nd of Neveruary."

Stephanie interrupts their banter. "If y'all are done flirting, can we get down to business cousin."

"Cousin!? Aw shit. It must be serious if you're calling me cousin." He lets out a sigh. "What's the problem?"

Stephanie explains the situation from the beginning. Starting with what happened at the gas station and ending with them arriving at his door. LaVar's initial look of concern changes to confusion then frustration and finally ending in anger as she finishes the story. He tries to keep cool despite his obvious deep irritation with the situation. "Let me get this straight. You stupid bitches pick up a gun with bodies on it, that you saw get the bodies on it, then beat and kidnap a kid on her birthday, then shoot a nigga in the dick with same gun with bodies from earlier, and now you show up at my spot with the murder weapon to multiple cases, a fucking kid hostage, and asking me to help a bitch I hate." He looks out the window and sees Robin and N'vaeh in the car. "Y'all gotta be the dumbest bitches I ever met." He turns to face Nadia. "You the stupidest bitch of all. All this bullshit over a nigga who don't want you. I would have made you abort my seed too if I got a dumb thot bitch like you pregnant."

Nadia slaps his mouth closed for making her remember how Davion hurt her. "Fuck You!"

LaVar returns the favor, slapping her so hard it knocks the earrings out of her ear. "Don't look shocked. I ain't the one to let nobody just slap me. I believe women deserve to get they ass whooped too."

Nadia pulls the gun out from her shirt and points it at LaVar. "And I believe men that hit women deserve to be shot."

Stephanie jumps between them and faces Nadia with her arms out. "NaNa please don't do this. He's right we already fucked up. We need to just get out of here and go on our way." She reaches for the gun slowly.

"Yeah bitch. Put that shit down and get the fuck up outta here." LaVar says as he closes the gap between him and Nadia.

"LaVar! Shut the fuck up!" Stephanie yells over her shoulder to Lavar who is now pressing up against her hard enough to inch them both closer to Nadia. "Back up! I got this." He stops moving as Nadia moves the gun closer to his nose. "Nadia, give me the gun. He is not worth it. We still have to go see Davion." Nadia looks at Stephanie who is now holding the gun and releases her grip. LaVar takes the opportunity and punches Nadia in the face knocking her unconscious on the floor. Stephanie points the gun at him. "Stop. Why would you do that?"

"I told you. Women deserve to get they ass beat too, and this bitch put a gun in my face. She lucky I ain't still stomping her out." He turns his attention to Stephanie. "Didn't I just tell you about this bitch putting a gun in my face and you still pointing that thing at me." He slaps the gun out of her hands, and it falls under the table. He then pushes her on the couch and starts choking her. "I always hated this cousin shit. I hate your mama. I only played along with it because I thought you would have gave me some head by now but all you do is bring me headaches." He continues choking her and she is beginning to lose consciousness.

Nadia awakens and sees what's happening and grabs the revolver in LaVar's waistband, puts it to his head and pulls the trigger. "There goes your head." His body falls and Stephanie is frozen as drops of his blood trickle off of her cheek. Nadia grabs a rag and tosses it to her while she looks for the other gun. "Steph where is the other gun." She claps her hands which ironically snaps Stephanie out her stupor. "Wipe your face off and tell me where the other gun is."

Stephanie wipes her face as if she were still trying to preserve her make up. "It's under the table." Nadia looks under the table and discovers a small bag filled with hundred-dollar bills and a few pieces of expensive men's jewelry in addition to the gun. She tucks both in her shirt and hands Stephanie LaVar's gun. They clean themselves up, head out the door with the evidence, and get in the car.

Robin still teary eyed and now in the driver's seat. "What happened? Is everything ok? What did he say?" Nadia gets in the front seat and Stephanie gets in the back when Robin notices the bruises on Nadia's face and Stephanie's neck.

"Things didn't go as planned?" Nadia notices Robin's make up is running "And I see you are still all broken up."

"It's not that. I kinda believe N'vaeh. I think we should take her home." Robin looks at Stephanie who hasn't said a word or made eye contact since getting back into the car. "I think Stephanie might agree with me. Right Steph. We can talk about everything once we get everybody home." Stephanie remains silent.

"Fuck it. Let's drop the puppy off and get back to solving the issue at hand." Nadia lets out an exaggerated sigh. "Thankfully my mood is improving." Tapping the bounty she picked up from LaVar. "Where do you live puppy since I'm in such a good mood and will let you live." N'vaeh tells Robin where to go and they proceed to drop her off.

"If you are taking me home can someone untie me now."

Nadia looks back and sees that Stephanie is still in her catatonic state. "Not yet puppy. I don't trust you completely and Steph is still on mental break." She sees the gun still in Stephanie's hand and reaches for it. "You don't need that right now."

"Hold the fuck up! How do you have another gun, and you didn't give me my shit back." Robin exclaims half-jokingly. "A nigga sacrificed his life so that I could be protected and y'all, my ride or dies, still haven't told me what happened at LaVar's."

Nadia returns Moses' gun to Robin. "All you need to know right now is that we gotta little help." She flashed the bag with the cash in it.

"Say less girl." Robin smiles and Nadia winks back.

As they get close to N'vaeh's house her phone goes off repeatedly from Stephanie's bra. "Stephanie, would you please answer the phone or put it on silent or move or something." Nadia reaches back and grabs the phone. She reads the text messages and becomes enraged. "I knew this bitch was lying the whole time!" She scrolls through the last couple texts. "Davion been texting this hoe all types of shit. 'Happy b-day', 'take care of our baby', eggplant emojis and shit." The phone goes off again with the text 'cum see me'. She throws the phone at N'vaeh. "This ride ain't over yet. Take us back to Davion's right the fuck now!"

Robin passes N'vaeh's house and they drive toward Davion's. She can see Nadia seething as she starts to rotate the revolver on her weapon. "Let's not go ballistic. Are you sure you still want to go over there like this."

"Ride or die…" Silence is heard after Nadia speaks. She speaks louder with more authority. "Ride or Die!"

"Until the day we die." Stephanie finally speaks up.

"Ride or die!" Nadia reiterates.

"Until the day we die!" The trio says with resounding confidence.

As they ride down Davion's block, they notice three of his underlings on the porch in an aggressive posture and when they get close, they start shooting at the car immediately hitting Robin in the head causing the car to creep to a crash directly in front of his house. Nadia grabs Robin's gun and jumps out the car shooting both of them instantly hitting one of the cronies. The other two try to take cover but can't find any.

In the backseat of the car, Stephanie is shot but still conscious. N'vaeh whispers to Stephanie just loud enough to be heard between the gun fire. "Please just untie me."

Nadia runs out of bullets from the revolver, but she picks up the gun from the first goon she shot. She catches the last two as they huddled up by the porch. She turns around to see the car door open with both of her friends dead inside. She tries to hold their lifeless bloody bodies but lets out a scream. She stands up and checks her guns. "This is all that puppy's fault."

SARGE

Sarge awakens to the footsteps of his mother shuffling to the bathroom and takes it as his cue to prepare for the day before she can command the rest of his morning. He checks the bed and is disappointed to find his emergency flask is bone dry and the shakes are starting to take effect. He reaches for a glass of water, but he can't control the vibrations long enough to take a big drink, so he grasps the cup with both hands and accepts the splashes that hit his mouth as a reward. The flushing of the toilet is his cue to pee in the basement sink so that his mother can't hear that he is awake. He sits on the edge of the bed trying to quench his thirst while he waits for his mother to settle herself back to sleep. He checks the clock once it's quiet again, 4:30am, and decides it's safe to leave and not too early to start the day. He follows a routine as if he were preparing for war. He gets suited and booted in what's left of his army gear from his discharge decades earlier. He grabs his flask, Swiss army combat knife, poncho, walking stick and tries to covertly get up the stairs and exit the basement.

"Who is that?" His mother yells thwarting his escape.

"It's just me Ma." He responds as he puts his head down in defeat.

"I need you to take the trash to the curb."

"Yes ma'am." Sarge says resisting the urge to remind her that garbage pickup isn't until tomorrow.

"I don't know why you try to sneak out of here so early when you know I might need you to do something. I took care of your butt for almost 50 years and now it's my turn for some get back." She says with consternation, indignation, and then a smile.

Sarge cedes before confrontation. "You right Ma. Do you need anything before I leave because I won't be back for a few hours?"

She pauses for a moment. "Well, I don't need anything right now but when you come back pick me up a chicken wing and a small slaw from KFC."

Sarge biting his tongue almost to the point where he is speaking in blood responds. "Yes ma'am." He lets out an exhausted sigh while he tries to figure out how he can get to KFC with no transportation, no money, and why she only wants one chickens wing.

She notices the sigh which enrages her. "Forget it then. I don't need shit from you. You just take your ass out there and find you a job so that you can get the hell out of my house!" She slams the door to the basement and goes to her room. Relief and regret wash over him. The relief that he can leave the house but the regret that he could not maintain his military bearing allowing her to see his true feelings.

He quickly takes the cans to the curb and disappears into the night. "Free at last." He says quietly turning the corner, while he prioritizes his morning. "First, collect bottles for anti-shake medicine and relax my mind as I patrol the neighborhood. Second, look for potential sources of income. Then meet up with the fellas at the seven o'clock store to see who got the best score. Then figure out how I'm going to get this damn chicken."

As he travels his normal route by the scrapyard to see if there is anything quick and easy to grab to resell to them after they open, he sees Doris muttering to herself across the street. "I know that ho stroll anywhere. Please don't let her see me." He says under his breath while trying to blend into the shadows. Luckily, she doesn't notice him as she travels in the opposite direction. "That was close. I don't have time for her begging ass right now." He gazes off into the distance remembering a time almost forgotten. "But damn, she was that deal back in the day." He bites his lip as he dives deeper in the memory. "That pretty skin, tight little body, crazy-sexy-cool attitude, and that voice. Ooh that voice was just so sweet in my ear."

"Crack-crack-crack crack-crack." Sarge hears faintly as the figure appears behind him.

Sarge snaps back to reality not realizing that Doris had seen him and double backed to catch up with him. Her words the reminder as to why she fell off so hard but despite the fall she still looked good. "What's up Doris? What you doing out so early?"

"You know what I'm doing silly. Don't act brand new. Let me hold a couple dollars." She says without skipping a beat.

"Now Doris, don't you see me out here with a bag of bottles. What makes you think I got money for you when I ain't got money for myself?" Sarge smiles while retorting.

"I know you gone get some money later just let me get those bottles for now. I'll make it worth your while." She says while reaching for his crotch and trying to kiss him on the neck.

Sarge swiftly uses his stick to create space between them. "Back up! Those days are over. Plus, I don't know where your mouth has been, but I got a good idea and I don't want no parts of that mouth...or ass...or pussy." He knows this is a lie but he can't be weak. "Just keep moving on your stroll and you'll get all the money you need."

"Fuck you Sarge! If you can't give me some money then take responsibility for your daughter. You ain't never did shit for her not once."

"That little girl can be anybody's in the neighborhood that had $5 or half pint. I don't know why you keep trying to put that baby on me." He vehemently responds.

"I'm not trying to do anything. We both know that I was only with you then."

"Whatever. Stop lying. I don't have any money for you and I'm not getting any for you either. As a matter of fact, you should be back paying me for all that dick I gave you when you were still worth something." He winces a little as he realizes what he just said but he must maintain the tough exterior or she will harp on his sympathy. "Now keep it moving and let me be."

"Whatever, whatever." She says in a sing song tone. "I don't need you, when all you do, is be boo boo."

Sarge already walking away. "I'll dismiss myself. Goodbye!"

"You can say whatever you want but I know you still love me." She says to Sarge's back as he walks away seemingly unscathed by her words.

Sarge mentally regroups and gets back to the task at hand. "Where is that hole in the fence?" He scans the area that normally provides him access to the scrapyard which seems to be missing. "I must be getting old or did they finally fix the gate?" He eyes the entire length of the fence for confirmation. "Shit!" He exclaims with subdued breath. "I was saving this for the trip to the store." He reaches in his pocket and pulls out a crumpled cigarette butt with, as he likes to say, 'a lot of meat on it' straightens it out and places it in his mouth. He reaches for his lighter cradling his walking stick while contemplating his next move. He must decide if he is going to jump the barbwire fence or try to collect bottles in the wake of Doris's stroll. He pauses right before the flame hits the remnant of the presmoked Newport 100 as he notices a rug by a tree next to the fence. "I love when god smiles down on me." He says while returning the butt to his pocket postponing his victory breathing treatment. He grabs his walking stick and tosses it over the fence as he prepares the rug for maximum safety and reliability. His first attempt to climb the tree did not go as planned because he forgot that after not jumping for over 10 years his vertical leap had diminished substantially. "Got Damn It!" He grunts to himself as he hits the ground. "I'm definitely getting old." He picks himself up without dusting off and climbs the gate while using the tree. He carefully lowers himself on the ground after successfully traversing the rug covered barbwire. "Too easy." He whispers as he temporarily basks in his 'old age' athleticism. He regains his focus and walking stick then stealthily searches for the aluminum. "When did they start rearranging and organizing shit like this!?" He says with confusion as he stumbles across some catalytic converters and copper wire. "Whatever." He shrugs. "Works for me." He starts to collect his bounty when he hears the unmistakable sound of animal paws striking the gravel. He readies himself because he can only hear the direction the unseen beast is coming from. He tries to grab the wire and run but is stopped immediately by the loudest bark and growl he had ever heard. The hound from hell stopped so suddenly that some of the gravel flew into Sarge's shin causing him to drop the wire and sprint towards the covered section of the gate. The demon spawn waited a moment before giving chase as if Sarge's fear made him stronger. A few steps away from the fence the creature of carnivorous carnage roars a 'BARK' which stops Sarge from throwing his walking stick over the fence. Instead, Sarge instinctively spins around striking what he believes to be death in canine form across the head. To his dismay, Satan's beastie catches then yanks the stick from his hands right before crushing it into two useless pieces. Sarge only heard the snap because he was in the process of miraculously hurling himself over the fence to safety. He catches his breath while leaning on the tree as his tormentor returns to the shadows. "That was too close for comfort." He looks up towards the sky. "Ok. That was a good one. I guess I needed to know that I wasn't getting too old. Lesson learned." He reaches in his pocket and is relieved to see that he still has his celebratory breathing treatment and smiles with the satisfaction of a loss well gained. Sarge finishes the butt and returns to his quest for bottles.

After a more than usual grueling collection of 10cent increments of trash/treasure (a matter of perspective) due to the Olympic performance he gave earlier, Sarge finally arrives at the seven o'clock store. He quickly assesses the situation taking note of the haul from the others and determines that he will have enough to stop the shakes that have unfortunately become more prominent now that the adrenaline has worn off and get the coveted 'chicken wing and small slaw'.

Sarge approaches the crew (Baghdad, Candyman, Stack-a-Dollars, and Catfish.) "At ease maggots. Have no fear, because Sarge is here." He sets down his bags of bottles next to his reserved two stacked crate throne.

Candyman jumps to his feet and renders a salute. "AH-TIN-HUT! Private Candyman reporting for drinking duty, sir!" The group starts laughing and sitting up straight while Candyman stands motionless.

"If you see a tin hut you burn it!" Sarge retorts with a tight-lipped smirk. "And don't call me sir! I work for a living." His faux scowl and rigid finger shift from Candyman's face to the rest of the crew who have begun to break character and gather their contributions. "You scum know what to do. Let's take this shit in the store, get our shit to drink, and then talk shit while we drink it. Understood!?"

"Sir, yes sir!" Candyman says forcefully while

maintaining his salute and the others fake haste. "Permission to put my hand down and help my fellow comrades with drinking, oh great and powerful Sarge."

Sarge unable to maintain his military demeanor explodes into laughter. "Alright you win, you dirty rotten scoundrel. Permission granted." As if on cue, the store's door chime signaling the opening of the store. His laughter fades into a personal chuckle as he gathers his bottles with increasingly shaking hands.

The light banter continues as the crew file into the store. Each giving the clerk a hard time as they barter for cheaper prices or get out of paying the debts for the days when they were 'a little short'. After the deals are made with promises of light janitorial services or another round of 'I got you next time' they head back to the parking lot to reap the bounties of their labors.

"I told your big ass they wasn't going to take those dirty ass bottles." Candyman says to Baghdad as he slaps the pack of Smoker's Choice cigarettes against his palm.

"Man, fuck you and your scratchy throat mothafucka. When I clean them bitches off and get something to drink, don't come begging." Baghdad says setting the plastic bags of bottles on the ground.

"Fuck you, you snaggle toothed gorilla. That's how a man's voice sound when he got teeth." Candyman quips back.

Sarge intervenes before the insults become serious. "Fuck both of y'all. You take this." He hands Baghdad his freshly opened half pint of 'rot gut' and then turns to Candyman. "And you let me get one of them brown boys." Candyman passes Sarge the cigarette he was about to light.

Baghdad refuses the liquor and points to the beer in Stack-a-Dollars' hand. "I want that."

Stack-a-Dollars takes a sip of the ice-cold malt liquor and adjusts his hat. "You ain't got enough money or pussy to get all this pretty right here."

"Nigga you know I mean the fucking beer, you negative ho pimp." Baghdad reaches for the can.

"You know I take care of all my bitches but next time say please or I'll have your big ass on Joy Rd. doing a ho stroll." Stack-a-Dollars says, earning a round of laughter from the group.

"Whatever nigga." Baghdad takes a big gulp accepting defeat in this round of insults before passing the beer to the next man in rotation.

The men continue to trade insults, share vices, and intermittently panhandle to keep the party going, when Benny Harman and Orangello arrive in Benny Hardman's old pickup truck. Sarge sees an opportunity to get a ride to KFC.

"What up my people." Benny Harman says while giving handshakes and fist bumps to the group. "I see y'all got the party started without us." Sarge hands him a half pint after shaking his hand.

"Speak for yourself." Orangello pulls a fifth of cheap vodka out of his pants. "I am the party." He takes a huge swallow and passes it down the line. "Don't drink all my shit or we gone have some problems."

"We all contribute here and you know this." Sarge says slightly offended by the comment. "If you can't be cool then take your shit and leave."

"You know I'm just playing Sarge."

"I might laugh and joke but I don't play." Sarge says with conviction.

An awkward silence falls upon the group until Mookie, one of the neighborhood bottom-feeder-crackheads, arrives on the scene. "What up fellas? What y'all getting into?" He says while sizing up the scene.

"You see what we getting into." Sarge says without changing position.

"Oh. Okay. Let me get a swig of what y'all sippin' on." Mookie advances toward the nearest drink.

"You didn't put in on nothing and you ain't got never got nothing to add to the pot. So, keep it pushing." Sarge commands.

"Yall know I can't go in the store." Mookie explains.

"You shouldn't have kept getting caught stealing jackass." Orangello blurts out from the peanut gallery.

"Gimme the money and I'll go get whatever you want." Candyman sticks his hand out.

"I'm a little short can you throw me a little blessing to help me out." Mookie explains.

Candyman snickers and puts his hand down. "Just like I thought. I bet you ain't even got a single coin in your pockets."

"Yeah, you right." He smiles and nods in agreement. "Can I get those bottles then?" He gestures towards Baghdad's dirty bottle rejects.

"Hell fuck naw!" Baghdad exclaims. "I would let you clean 'em up and split it with you but your thieving ass will just disappear with the money. Plus, you can't even go in any store around here. So, what your dumb ass going to do with them shits."

"Somebody will take 'em in the store for me." Mookie says with confidence.

"No nigga!" Baghdad sighs. "Damn!"

"Anyways." Catfish interjects. "Orangello, ain't orangelo a fruit. Don't that make you a fruity ass nigga?"

"Shut your stankin ass up. Smell like you been eatin' Doris nasty perch pussy all week." Orangello fires at Catfish.

"Nope. Just your mama's." Catfish fires back before putting on a serious face. "But for real, where did your name come from?"

"Orangelo only got one L in it and my name got two." Orangello pauses for a moment. "My mom's favorite colors is orange and yellow and she said I looked like if the colors were combined when I was born. The end nigga." He takes a drink from his bottle and passes it off.

"Really?" Sarge says with a puzzled look before laughing hysterically.

Orangello scans the crew's response when he realizes that he gave the bottle to Mookie who has been guzzling it down the past few seconds. "That's what we doing?" He grabs the bottle from Mookie mid guzzle and examines how much is left. "It's like that." He gives the almost empty bottle to Benny Harman. "Hold this." He casually walks to the truck and grabs a pipe out the pile of scrap in the truck bed and walks back to the group. "This been a long time coming." He whacks him across the face splashing blood over the already soiled bottles and knocking him to the ground. He moves in for a second blow when Sarge steps between them.

"Put the pipe down. He's had enough." Sarge grabs Orangello's arms to restrain him.

"Fuck that! This nigga drank damn near all my liquor. Always stealing and begging and shit." Orangello pushes forward but Sarge maintains control forcing his attention to Sarge. "Let me go Sarge. I gotta fuck him up."

"He's already fucked up." Sarge releases his grip on one arm and reaches in his pocket. "Here take this." He tries to hand Orangello the money he saved for his mother's KFC order. "This should make you whole." He lets go of the other arm forcing the money into Orangello's hand.

Orangello looks over Sarge's shoulder and takes the money. "For you Sarge. I'll let it ride this time. But next time you see Mookie tell him he owe you."

Sarge turns around to see the pool of blood as the only trace of Mookie. "Where did he go that fast?"

"You know you can't keep them type of crackheads down for long. Can You?" Candyman says giving elbow nudges to Catfish's side.

Sarge puts his head down in defeat and walks off.

"Where you headed Sarge?" Candyman asks.

"Away. I'll be back after a while." Sarge decides to go back to the junkyard to try and get the scrap he left behind so that he can still get the chicken.

Sarge takes the journey back to the junkyard replaying the events at the store wondering how he let things escalate so far, when he sees Davion walking towards him squinting and rubbing his eyes. "Hey Nephew, what's wrong with your eyes?"

"Nothing. Don't worry about it." Davion stops wiping his face to show he's fine. "I was just coming to find you."

"What you need Nephew? You know I'll look out for

you." Sarge sees an opportunity to catch two birds with one stone.

"I need you to do me a favor and introduce Moses to the crew and get them familiar with him. Make sure they know to show him the same respect they show me. I'm trying to show him the value of having 'friends' in low places. He's going to be running things around here for me and he doesn't know how important you fellas are to the organization. To be honest, I don't think any of y'all know."

"Too easy. I can school another young pup."

"I'll school him you just make sure the others accept him." Davion says curtly.

Sarge's enthusiasm fades. "No problem, but you think you can give me a few dollars so I can get Ma her chicken and slaw? I had the money b..."

Davion interrupts. "'Too easy.' Aren't those the words you used?" He reaches in his pocket to grab the money.

"Thank you, Son." Sarge realizes his mistake in his moment of sincere gratitude and tries to correct it. "I mean Nephew."

Davion's expression disappears and his search for money changes to a revealing of his pistol. He grabs Sarge by the throat and presses the gun to his eyebrow. His voice low and pointed. "I allow you to call me Nephew out the kindness in my heart but don't mistake it for forgiveness. I've told you once to NEVER call me that again." He presses the gun deeper into his brow and tightens his grip around his throat. Each word accentuated with increased pressure to his skull. "EVER! Or I. WILL. KILL. YOU." He unclenches his teeth, releases his grip slightly and allows Sarge's head to return to a neutral position. "Are we clear?" Sarge tries to nod with his eyes. "Say the words. Are we clear?"

"We're clear." Sarge squeezes the words out while still trying to breathe.

"Good." Davion releases him and puts his gun away. He reaches for and hands Sarge $10. "Get Ma her food and get yourself something to make you forget that word when you see me."

Sarge begrudgingly accepts as he attempts to regain his composure. "Thanks Nephew."

"Don't forget. I'm going to bring Moses around in about an hour or so. So be at the store with your crew and take care of him."

Sarge nods in agreement as they go their separate ways.

Sarge walks to a different liquor store to regroup before heading back to the crew. After getting his drinking legs back he notices a cable truck open and some copper wire ready for the taking. He looks up at the sky. "I knew you didn't forget about me." As he is about to grab the spool, he hears someone approaching rapidly. He tries to play it off like he dropped something under the truck.

"You know I can see you right." The technician speaks as Sarge begins to rise and face him.

"I was looking for my quarter. I think it rolled underneath your truck." Sarge says confidently.

"If you say so." The technician says with a disbelieving grin. "People love to steal wire. I thought you might be one of those people."

"Never that. I'm too old to be carrying all that around. The heaviest thing I like to carry is this." Sarge holds up his half pint and takes a drink.

"I'll tell you what. If you leave the quarter, I'll give you this bag I got from my customer." He hands Sarge a dime bag of what looks like marijuana. "He said it's a little extra in there so be careful or sell it."

Sarge grabs the bag and places it in his pocket. "This dime is worth way more than quarter. I appreciate ya'. Have a blessed day." Sarge exits before the technician changes his mind.

"Goodluck." The technician says as he closes the back of the truck.

Sarge continues his trek back to familiar territory, hoping Benny Harman is still at the store so that he could get a ride to KFC. He sees Doris approaching rapidly with a sloppy gait. "Aw shit. Here we go again." He says to himself aloud. He notices that she isn't her happy go lucky self and decides to entertain her for a little bit but she speed stumbles past him like he isn't there. "Where you going sweetheart? You acting like you don't know me no more."

She stops dead in her tracks. "Shut up!" She looks him up and down until she recognizes him. "Sarge. I'm taking my ass home, with your nosy ass."

Sarge waves the half pint like he's hypnotizing her. "Don't you wanna tell me what's wrong with you?"

"Gimme that shit." She tries to snatch the bottle but Sarge pulls away in time.

He takes the bag off the bottle and hands it to her. "Wipe all that shit off your mouth first."

She wipes the vomit and blood off her face and then throws the bag on the ground. "You happy now." She holds out her hand. "Now give it here." She takes the bottle and drinks it.

Sarge snatches out her hand before she drinks too much. "Alright that's good. Now tell me what's going on."

"Punk ass Davion boys. Them bitch ass niggas, the 3J's, put they hands on me."

"What for?" Sarge says pretending not to know its crack related.

"It don't matter what for. I'm a fucking woman and ain't no man 'pose to put his hands on a woman."

"You might be a female, but I don't know about no woman." Sarge says smiling while passing her the liquor.

"Fuck you Sarge. You wasn't saying that all those years ago."

"You know I'm just playing girl. You right though. Davion needs to keep his goons in check. It's no reason to beat on no woman, no matter how much they deserve it."

"It ain't over yet. I still owe him some money and I have to get it to him today." She takes another sip and passes it back to Sarge.

"I can't believe that boy is my son. Allowing that shit to happen." Sarge says nonchalantly.

"Davion is your son!?" She says taken aback. "Bullshit! Since when?"

"Never mind. Don't ever say that shit again. It's just between me and you."

"Fuck that. Tell that nigga to let me slide if he is your son."

"I'm serious." Sarge looks deep into her eyes. "Don't say shit to nobody about our connection. We ain't like that with each other and he don't listen to me anyways."

Doris sees the seriousness in his eyes. "Well then, you give me some money or you might not see my ass no more."

"I ain't got it." He says while trying to pass her the last of the liquor. "This is all I can do."

She takes the bottle and starts to walk off. "Fuck you

then. You just a deadbeat dad to two children. I'll just get my daughter to help me out."

"I mean it Doris. Don't say shit to anybody." Sarge says as she gives him the middle finger and stagger steps away.

Sarge finally gets back the 7 o'clock store and is grateful to see Benny Harman is still there. KFC is finally open and he has enough money to get the chicken wing, small slaw, and a biscuit for good measure. Candyman stands up to salute but Sarge waves him off. "Sorry gentleman. No time for pleasantries." He turns to Benny Harman. "You think you can take me to get some chicken for Ma."

"You ain't even gotta ask. You know I'm going to take you to get moms some chicken." Benny Harman gets in the truck immediately followed by Sarge.

Benny Harman drops Sarge off at home. "You going in and out or you gone stay here for a while?"

"Don't worry about it. I'll meet y'all up there in a minute."

"Alright. Tell moms I said hello and I took your ass to get her chicken." Benny Harman pulls off before Sarge can respond.

Sarge enters the house to his mother's voice. "Who is that?"

"It's me Ma. I don't know why you think a burglar has keys?"

"Shut up boy. You know I get scared being in here all

by myself. Did you get the chicken?"

Sarge hands her the bag and her face lights up. "Of course, Ma."

"You're such a good boy." She tears off the drum from the wing as a reward. "Here, you can have this."

"Ma, you only have one chicken wing. You need to eat that." Sarge thinks about the tribulations he went through to get this chicken and bites his tongue as he remembers the smile on her face when he handed her the bag.

"Just take it." Anger almost escapes as he lectures her but the smell keeps her spirits high. "It's good." She opens the slaw. "You want some slaw?"

"The chicken is more than enough. Thanks Ma." He turns to leave the bedroom.

"Try not to be gone all day. You know I get lonesome."

Sarge, out of her sight, grimaces then wipes it away with his hand. "Yes ma'am."

Sarge returns to the crew refreshed and eager to enjoy the rest of his day when he sees Davion approaching with new nephew. "Hey Catfish, put this to good use." He tosses the bag of weed+ to Catfish.

Catfish examines the bag with glee. "You ain't gotta tell me twice." He reaches for his rolling papers.

"Don't put it all that in there. It's got something extra in it." Sarge says with a wink.

"Alright, no problem but I'm a add a little bit of this to it." Catfish pulls out a small baggie of crack.

"Whatever floats your boat." Sarge shrugs off the additional additions to the weed and focuses on the task at hand. "My mouth is dry and I got a cognac taste and a vodka budget." He tries to lighten his thoughts with humor and ease his mind with alcohol.

"I gotcha Sarge." Candyman hands him a bottle of Arrow vodka. "Just what the doctor ordered."

Sarge laughs before he takes a sip. He begins to feel relaxed as the burning liquid hits the half chicken wing in his stomach. "I needed that." He sticks his hand out and presents the bottle for the next one in rotation.

"Don't mind if I do." Baghdad says when he sees Candyman reaching for the bottle.

Sarge feeling confident again regains his control of the group and starts telling a story of his 'glory' days in the field, when Davion interrupts his spiel. "Stop all that lying! Sarge, I thought honor was the corner stone of your character."

Sarge panics internally for a moment but remembers all he has to do is welcome the new nephew and everything should be alright. (But more importantly. When is Catfish going to be done rolling up?)

HEAVEN'S GATE

N'vaeh wakes up looks around her room and smiles, despite being home alone on her birthday. She grins to herself as she looks over the shithole she calls home. She undauntingly reflects on the fact she can't go to Harvard even though she was accepted months ago as she spots the acceptance letter and list of possible grants. She chuckles to herself as she enters the bathroom and begins to wretch at the smell of vomit, shit, and whatever else comes with having a crackhead mother on a bender. She cleans up the mess and readies herself for the day when she catches her own eyes in the mirror and beams before exclaiming, "Happy Birthday to me!" She takes a deep breath and lets out a slow exhale closing her eyes and says quietly still smiling, "I made it. I'm almost free." She opens her eyes eager to check the emancipation paperwork she's been preparing for months now that she is legally old enough to file for it when she hears the door open with force.

"N'vaeh get in here right now!" The smell of her

evening entering the room before the sound of her voice. "Mommy needs you."

N'vaeh instantly recognizes the tone and the joy she had a moment ago is replaced by the disgust she has for her mother's life choices. "What is it now?!" She blurts out without regard for her tone.

"Who the fuck do you think you talking to like that? Come the fuck here before I beat the dumb back in that smartass mouth." Her mother claps in concurrence with her slurred words.

"Here I come." N'vaeh responds humbly before following her mother's command.

Her mother changes her demeanor back to motherly when N'vaeh enters the room. "You know I love you with all my heart and mommy would never do anything to really hurt you right?"

"Um. If you say so." She says with disbelief as she braces for impact.

Mother rolls her eyes and smacks her lips. "Anyway, as I was saying." Her tone changes again to demanding. "Mommy is going to need you to do that special favor you did before."

N'vaeh's face goes cold "No. You said I would never have to do anything like that again." The tears in her eyes begin to swell as she remembers the last time she had to do a 'special favor' for her mother or more importantly her mother's 'friend'. "I can't do anything like that again. I just can't."

There is a knock at the door. "Who is it?" she yells at the door before looking at N'vaeh. "Get up and go see who at the door." N'vaeh obeys before she allows a tear to fall down her face. When she opens the door, she sees a large envelope in the door and grabs it. "Who's at the door?" her mother yells with a hint of fear in her voice.

N'vaeh's tear is dried when she recognizes the maize and blue of the University of Michigan. "Nobody, it's just the mailman." She begins to open the letter.

"Mailman don't usually run this early." She says slightly confused but more relieved. "Is it more of that school shit? I don't know why they keep sending this shit. Don't they know you ain't going to no college no time soon. You have obligations you have to take care of."

"Like what. Sucking dick to pay off your crack debts." Mother slaps N'vaeh. "I'm still not doing it." N'vaeh tries to leave the room but her mother grabs her arm. "Let me go!" N'vaeh snatches away and continues to her room and slams the door with her mother close behind.

Mother tries to force the door open but N'vaeh was fast enough to lock the door. "Open the door." She starts pounding on the door demanding to be obeyed before switching to pleas. "Please honey, I need you to do this for me one last time." She begins to sob. "Davion is not like the last guy. He is not going to take it easy on me. He is going to kill your mother. Do you want your mother to die? Please help your mother."

N'vaeh allows her mother's pleas to creep into her conscience as she finishes reading the full four-year scholarship acceptance letter from UofM. "How much do you owe?" she says begrudgingly.

"Three hundred." Mother hears shuffling around. "What are you doing in there? Just come out so we can talk."

The door opens and N'vaeh throws the money at her mother. "Here. Take it. Now never ask me for anything ever again." She says looking at her like she was talking directly to her soul.

Her mother responds smugly as she picks up the money. "Ok thanks, but you still didn't do what I told you to do. You obviously don't have a problem with it if you have all this money." She says while uncrumpling the bills. "We can call this back rent. Now go on over to Davion's and make mama proud." Her eyes are shining looking at the new money in her life.

"I already told you. I owe you nothing because you are nothing." She holds up the letter. "This is all I needed to get a new life away from you."

Mother laughs. "You can't go nowhere without me saying so cause you still just a kid. I don't care how much of a genius them schools think you is." She grabs the letter, tears it up and throws it on the ground. "Now where you going to go?" N'vaeh stares blankly at her mother emotionless. "I'll tell you since you acting all quiet and shit. You are going to take that young pussy to Davion and let him do whatever he want and then we gone find some other niggas to use that body up before you do. After that, then maybe you can take your smart ass to college."

N'vaeh blinks and a moment later she finds herself attacking her mother ferociously. The years of torment are taken out on her mother in a matter of a minutes. Her mother not being in any condition to fight back gets manhandled. During the struggle Mother grabs a broom to try and stop the beating but it was taken by N'vaeh who then proceeds to mount then choke her with the handle. N'vaeh listens to mother struggle to get air and finally manages to speak in labored grunting breath. "I hate you. You never loved me. How could you do this to your own daughter?" She leans closer as she watches the light leave her mother's eyes. "Goodbye you." She collapses on her mother's body and whispers in her ear, "Happy birthday to me."

After the cathartic killing of her mother, N'vaeh realizes that she still has to deal with Davion let alone her mother's dead body. She cleans up the mess as best she could while panicking when she decides to kill two birds with one stone by paying Davion what her mother owed and then making it look like he killed her mother. She knew she needed to act fast, or it would be too difficult to blame someone else. She grabbed the money that her mother had and planned on talking Davion into coming back to her house to leave some evidence but not before dragging her mother's body to the back room.

N'vaeh arrives at Davion's only to discover that he is not home despite his car being parked there. She tries around the house checking various windows for activity to no avail. She checks the back door with no luck and finally decides that she needs to go home and rethink her plan. As she leaves the backyard, she notices a car with a group of females parked out front looking at her. She tries to ignore it when one of them gets out of the car and hits her in the face with a gun. She's dazed and confused as she keeps yelling stuff about 'Davion come get his bitch' and 'being pregnant or something' before being kicked in the stomach. The beating continues and N'vaeh becomes numb to the scenario attributing it to justice for what she did earlier. After being beaten and robbed by the three women they grab her and force her into the car claiming that they were taking her for a ride. N'vaeh believing that there is no way out of the situation awaits her fate and succumbs to the ride.

She maintains the serenity with the acceptance that she was going to die until she witnesses the slaying of Corey. At this moment she snaps out of it and sees that her story is not over yet. These women are not thinking clearly, and they will make a mistake at some point. She knows all she needs is the right opportunity. She believes that Robin is the key to her salvation because now she knows they have something in common. Her thoughts are so intense that she can barely hear what is going on around her until they reach the car.

Nadia's voice finally pierces through the noise of her mind. "Here give this to the puppy. She might be thirsty too."

"No thank you." N'vaeh vehemently denies the offering wanting to make sure that she can think clearly especially now that they are getting more intoxicated.

"Bitch. You don't have a choice. You gone learn not to bite the hand that feeds you." Nadia lashes out after the perceived disrespect.

"Just drink it. Pretend it's a birthday shot. I know it's your birthday today. I saw it on your phone." Stephanie holds up N'vaeh's phone. "If not, I can't promise this will end nice for you."

N'vaeh considers the fact that one shot could help give her some liquid courage and it might be her last day on earth otherwise. She nods slightly with her head and submits with her eyes.

"Tilt your head back." Robin grabs the bottle and begins to pour it into N'vaeh's mouth when the car jolts due to the reckless driving of Nadia. "Damn NaNa. You made me spill this shit on my backseat. Drive normal, nobody is chasing us." She finishes pouring the liquor in her mouth. "That wasn't so bad was it."

N'vaeh glares at Nadia as the rage begins to bubble from the burning liquid she just swallowed. "Not at all. Happy Birthday to me."

N'vaeh zones out again trying to adjust to the alcohol in her system when Nadia's voice pokes through again. "Come on Stephanie you know how he is. Let's get in here and figure this shit out." She says before turning her attention to Robin. "We shouldn't be too long. Just make sure the puppy stays quiet." Nadia and Stephanie immediately exit, and Robin's impenetrable façade is dropped again as she reminisces to herself.

N'vaeh sees her opportunity now that she is alone with Robin. "Can I have another drink of that?" She motions to the bottle with her head. "If you don't mind."

Robin shakes her head in disbelief "Really!? I don't think you can handle another one."

"What do I have to lose? I'm pretty sure Nadia's going to kill me and it's still my birthday. Remember?" She says in a calming voice.

"You right. Fuck it. I need another one too." Robin grabs the bottle. "You know the routine. Head back."

N'vaeh takes another gulp and winces when it goes down this time. "That one stung a lil bit." She chuckles as Robin joins her. N'vaeh takes advantage of Robin letting her guard down. "What happened?" she says with concern.

Robin's smile turns to a scowl. "You saw what happened. A hoe ass nigga got what he deserved. End of story."

"I'm not talking about in there." N'vaeh intensifies her stare into Robin's gaze ensuring maximum eye contact. "What <u>really</u> happened?" She continues without breaking eye contact.

"Are you deaf little girl? I just told." Her glossed over gaze begins to return. "He did wrong and he got what he deserved."

N'vaeh interjects before she loses her again. "It's written all over your face. Just let it out." She takes a deep breath and braces for impact as she tries to figure out what is going on in Robin's head. She exhales slowly as if trying to coach Robin through breathing exercises. "Come on. Look in my eyes. I see you. Just let it all out."

"I keep telling you the same shit but you ain't getting it. What? Do you need to hear how he used to tease me, every day, about how I dressed and who I played with when we were kids? How he used to smack me, punch me, spit on me, and pull my pants down mocking my 'big ass clit' in front of everyone. The names he used to call me, especially 'faggot ass Ru...'." She stops mid word as she gets lost in her memory.

N'vaeh tries to comfort yet encourage her to

continue. "And what happened next?"

Robin licks her lips and smiles but still stuck in her memories. "I left the city for a while and came back this confident pretty woman. I mean look at me who wouldn't want to be with me. And I see Corey. I know he doesn't recognize me and I see how I can pay him back for all those years of his bullshit." She takes a deep breath and continues the story. "So, I get his attention with my, you know, assets which he obviously can't resist and he invites me in the house. I set my phone on record and went in. We started making out and right before I was going to give him some head, I was going to tell him who I really was and show the video as proof." She looks up as if the incident was replaying in the air and shakes her head back and forth. "But things didn't go as planned. Right when I was about to pull his dick out, he whispered in my ear 'I know who you are and I don't want you to stop.' I can still feel and smell his terrible breath on my neck." She closes her eyes right before the tears fall. "I realize that if I do it, he still wins and I get up to leave. And that bitch ass coward ass pussy ass nigga hit me in the back of the head. And, and, and. Over and over again." Her words have grown to a roar. "FUCK HIM! FUCK HIM! FUCK HIM!" She trails off repeating the same words until she is just sobbing.

N'vaeh tries to lighten the mood while keeping her off balance. "I think it's time for another shot."

Robin releases a wet snort with a chuckle. "You

must be related to Oprah or something. Got me opening up and ugly crying about some dead piece of shit." She opens and takes a sip from the bottle. "I ain't never told nobody about that. Not even my girls. The only other person that knew is a dickless corpse." She looks at N'vaeh playfully. "And now you." Her face changes to stern seriousness. "If you even mention this to anyone, ever, ON GOD you already know the consequences. Are we clear?"

"I understand. I see you." N'vaeh says while nodding in agreement.

Robin back in control of her emotions starts to wipe her face. "Look at all this. I need to fix my face." She gets out of the car and back in the front seat.

N'vaeh feels that she's losing the potential to get free leaving as Robin gets further away from untying her physically. "What about that birthday shot for me?"

"Um, I think you've had enough young lady. I don't need you throwing up in my car."

N'vaeh realizes that she is losing the connection with Robin and decides to share with as much sincerity as possible. "It's ok. I don't need any more anyway. I just want the day to be over. I woke up with a future full of possibilities then my mom destroyed that. But not before offering my body to her drug dealer to pay her debts...again. Can you believe she wanted to take my money and pimp me out until I turned 18? I decide to pay her debts with my school money and get kidnapped in the process.

Now I might die and my mom not once wished me a happy birthday."

Robin pauses with cleaning her face as she becomes convinced that N'vaeh is actually the victim. "I'm sorry that all this is happening especially on your birthday. I wish we could start this whole day over... except the Corey part, but we can't. I'm really, really sorry N'vaeh."

Upon hearing Robin call her by name, N'vaeh is positive she is just moments away from freedom. "How about you," she raises her tied hands before she continues but Robin gets distracted by a visibly shaken Nadia and Stephanie returning to the car. N'vaeh puts her head down and says to herself. "So close."

Fortunately for N'vaeh she was able to get through to Robin who convinces her cohorts to finally grant her release and even take her home. Now that one problem is solved, she needs to figure out what to do about her mother while her captors are focused on their next string of crimes. Unfortunately, the text messages she received from Davion came at the worst time putting her back at square one and her dreams of freedom were taken away yet again.

They arrive at Davion's to an apparent ambush. After Robin is shot in the head and Nadia exits the vehicle guns blazing, N'vaeh sees what her last chance might be to get out of this alive.

Stephanie is shot, conscious and frozen in fear. N'vaeh whispers to Stephanie just loud enough to be heard between the gun fire. "Please just untie me." Stephanie remains motionless bleeding from her wound and staring into oblivion. N'vaeh picks up the liquor bottle and commences to beating Stephanie in the head until the bottle breaks. She tries to use the glass shards to cut the straps binding her, but the blood makes it almost impossible. She decides to make a run for it, opens the door and begins to run down the street when she hears a deafening scream from Nadia. She tries to avoid her line of sight and runs down the alley.

Nadia sees N'vaeh just as she turns in the alley and checks her guns. "This is all that puppy's fault." She races off toward the alley on foot covered in her friend's blood.

Sarge who has been drinking heavily since his stoop buddies and pseudo nephew were killed earlier, needs to relieve himself in the alley by the dumpster. As he prepares to urinate, N'vaeh crashes into him trying to seek a hiding place behind the dumpster. "Are you all right sweetheart?" He says with concern as he notices her condition and the panic in her face.

"She's trying to kill me." Is the only thing that N'vaeh has the wind for as she tries to catch her breath and stay hidden. "Can you please help me with these straps."

"Calm down. I got you. Don't worry. I don't see

anybody coming." He starts untying the straps. He is just finishing when he looks at N'vaeh and can see the fear in her face and spins around just before Nadia shoots him. Sarge falls to the ground keeping himself on top of N'vaeh to protect her. "Please don't do this. You are not a killer. It doesn't have to be like this." Sarge is determined not to let another person die on him today. "If you have to kill someone, shoot me. Just let the little girl go. I beg you."

Nadia still intent on killing N'vaeh. "Move unc this don't have nothing to do with you. This puppy needs to be put down."

Sarge pleads again. "You are too young to put yourself in this situation. Please don't." He sees her begin to squeeze the trigger and tries to cover N'vaeh as much as possible when he hears the gun shot. "Nooo!" He screams holding her motionless body as a pool of blood forms beneath them. Nadia drops to her knees because its finally over.

DAVION LEGREL

Early in the morning, Nadia is in bed grinning with her legs against the wall while Davion is in the bathroom. Davion loudly and angrily. "Nadia! What the fuck did you do?" He looks at the nearly empty condom.

Nadia innocently responds. "What's wrong bae?" Davion's phone vibrates and Nadia investigates.

He sees that the tip is missing. "Stop playing stupid. I'm looking at the big ass hole in this condom you brought that you just had to put on me with your mouth." He says under his breath. "This bitch is out her fucking mind." He calms down when he remembers the last time he slipped up and grabbed the 'plan b' he kept for just such an emergency. He comes out of the bathroom and tries to hand her the pill. "No worries. Just take this and all is forgiven."

Nadia slaps his hand away. "Get the fuck out of here with that shit and focus on what bitch is texting you at this time. You need to unlock this phone and show me all the messages." She shows him his phone with an unread message.

Davion not willing to hide his frustration another second erupts. "Why the fuck are you going through my phone? Why the fuck do you think we are together? And why in the motherfucking world would I ever want a baby with your crazy ass? We fucked twice that's it! Then you pull this psycho bitch shit, cutting holes in condoms and going through my phone trying to check me and shit." He snatches the phone then steadies his tone. "Now you can either take this pill and chill out or you can take this pill and get the fuck out. The choice is yours."

Nadia engulfed in rage slaps Davion across the face. "Fuck you!" She sees that he is unphased which makes her go into a frenzy. Davion avoids the wild swings and grabs her close, pinning her arms between them. Nadia resorts to spitting in his face.

"I see you chose option two." He wrestles her back to the bed, mounts her and forces the pill in her mouth and keeps his hand there. "Swallow it and I'll let you up." Nadia struggles pointlessly for a moment then relaxes her body. "Are you going to behave?" She nods in acquiescence and swallows. He removes his hand and gets up. "See. That wasn't so bad." He grabs her things and tosses them by her. "This is the last time we ever fuck. Now put your clothes on and leave."

Nadia sits up and nods her head in agreement repeatedly as she gets dressed muttering. "Ok. I got you. No problem. I see the games you wanna play."

Davion barely makes out the words she is saying. "Games. You talking about games." He laughs while he checks the message on his phone.

Nadia returns to her previous state of rage. "How you gonna check that shit in front of me." She pulls out her mace and maces him.

"Really!?" Davion squinting grabs Nadia who is kicking and screaming and forces her out the door. She clings to the doorframe and the pain from the mace is starting to affect his judgement so he kicks her out the door and she falls down the stairs. He slams the door and applies first aid to his face while Nadia cries on the ground and then gets up and leaves.

After agonizing with the mace for a while, he hears a knock at the door. Rubbing his eyes he goes to the door. "Who!" he yells.

"It's Doris." The voice on the other side responds demurely.

He opens the door barely able to make out crackhead Doris. "Why are you knocking on my door?"

Doris responds in an Usher style song and dance to match. "Its seven o'clock, on the dot, I need a crack rock, coming from you." She finishes and sticks out her hand to be rewarded for her performance. Davion stares at her with contempt. "Come on Davion, I need a little hook up."

"Why the fuck would you come to my house asking about some rocks. You know where to go."

"Jabari and them told me to come holler at you cause I was a little short." She says in her sweetest voice.

He shakes his head. "Got damn 3Js." He focuses back on Doris. "Look. I can't help you. If Jabari, Joe, or Jeff wanna look out for you, that's on them but that's as good as it gets from this house."

"Just let me hold a little something." She reaches for his crotch. "I can make you feel real good."

"Get out of here with nonsense. Ain't no way I want some of that old crack pussy." He starts to rub his eyes again.

"Well then my daughter can take care of you."

He looks at Doris and thinks for a minute about what she might have looked like before crack. "What's her Instagram? If she looks good then I might consider some kind of deal." He hands her his phone and she puts in N'vaeh's number.

"I don't know about all that instatwitter but I put her number in there."

Davion remembers that she only has one daughter. "Are you talking about your little girl? Isn't she like 15?" He snatches the phone back. "Get the fuck off my porch and don't ever come to my house again." He slams the door in her face then sits down and checks the message from earlier. "Bet. It's about time." He says aloud while starting to get dressed.

He calls Jabari and tells him that he needs to come over right now and then texts Moses that they should meet up in about an hour.

The 3Js arrive at Davion's house about ten minutes later and try to knock on the door but Davion opens the door beforehand. "Why the fuck are all three of y'all here? I told Jabari to get over here not you two. Who is at the spot?"

Jeff and Joe look at Jabari. "Crackhead Doris…"

Davion smacks him upside the head. "Why would you leave the spot with a crackhead in charge of crack?"

Jabari stammers. "You didn't let me finish." He points to Jeff. "We brought the stuff with us."

Davion smacks him again. "What is wrong with people bringing work to my house." He steps outside and leans close and with a stern quieted voice and clenched teeth. "First, Joe and Jeff get that shit off my property and back to the spot. Then get Doris out of there quietly." He pauses for a moment. "Don't tell me that you fuck boys spotted her some work either. Just make sure the money is right by this afternoon." He relaxes his posture slightly. "Do any of you have clean license?" Jabari nods. "Good. After you sort this shit out at the spot, take one of the other two and rent me an SUV with 4WD then meet me back here."

"Why you need a rental if you got a car?" Jabari ponders out loud.

"I'm taking a business trip and stop asking questions you should already know the answers to. Now stop wasting time and let's make this happen." Davion walks back into the house while the 3Js leave arguing amongst themselves about who 'fucked up' the most.

About a half hour later, Moses shows up and texts Davion that he is outside. Davion grabs his .45 leaves the house as Moses is walking up the walkway. "What's the plan big man?"

"Let's walk and talk. I have something I need to discuss with you." Davion says as he reaches Moses.

"No problem." Moses reaches for the prerolled blunt he has in jacket pocket. "If we smoking."

"Not this time. I have to stay levelheaded right now, but you can puff away." Davion says waving the blunt away.

"More for me." He lights the blunt and they start to walk towards the corner. "So, what's the situation?"

"I finally got the call from one of my boys from college on the next opportunity to set up shop and I need you to step up and handle things here while I'm gone." Davion says to a puzzled Moses. "Why do you look confused? We've been talking about this for months. Didn't I tell you how this works?" Unbeknownst to them, Nadia and her friends arrive on the block equally oblivious to the missed interaction.

Moses takes another drag holding in the smoke and speaks trying to keep it in. "Yeah, yeah, yeah. I know. You rob white drug dealers keep the cash and sell the product giving all the money to the crew." He exhales the rest of the smoke. "I'm tripping on the fact that you went to college."

Davion offended changes the direction of the conversation and his speech pattern. "Interesting. So, what do you need from life?"

"What any man wants. Money, power, respect. The usual shit expected with manhood."

Davion chuckles. "Is that it?"

"Oh yeah, the most important is the access to good pussy whenever and however I wanted it."

Davion shakes his head. "I'm disappointed. That's the type of answer I'd expect from any other nigga I met on the streets. I was hoping that you would be a little bit more specific and creative than the American dream force fed down our throats since our arrival in this country. It's like you're striving for mediocrity. Is it because I'm not a lawyer or a doctor is why you didn't fathom my post-secondary education?"

Moses slightly humbled. "I didn't mean it like that. Before now. You didn't sound like one of those college niggas."

"That's the problem with y'all and your misguided expectations of life outside the neighborhood.

Doctor, lawyer, athlete, entertainer, or drug dealer those are the only ways to get out but those are the limitations placed on us by our nurtured sense of an imaginary glass boiling pot called oppression. The best way out is in, through ownership."

"It might be the weed, but I don't get it."

"I'm doing it right now. I take money from other communities and feed it into ours turning as many people as possible into their own bosses." He clears his throat and smirks at Moses "Like you for example. I realize it may be a little illegal, but it is the best way I know how."

"You right. My bad you smart ass nigga." Moses says grinning as the last morsel of the blunt absorbs into his fingertips.

"Smart ass college nigga. You the smart-ass nigga and stop sucking that blunt like that or you might burst a capillary." Davion laughs after imagining the sight.

"The blunt is gone and we ain't there yet. What's the issue?" Moses says as they approach Sarge and his crew at the abandon church.

"Almost. We need to meet up with some important people."

"I hope you ain't talking about those drunks over there cause they just look like custos."

"Don't view them as bums. It's a mistake to dismiss them that easy. I realize that they are shadows of men but they have a wealth of knowledge and experience. A few big bad decisions got them to this point and a lot of good little decisions keep them going. Their contemporaries didn't make it this far with life and freedom. Nobody is more plugged into the neighborhood than them."

Moses retorts. "Like I said before. Why are we hanging around these bums? And please can you talk normal again. You made your point."

Davion continues. "Come on let me introduce you." They approach the group. The little one being the loudest, of course, preaches to the choir about his great deeds and magnificent sacrifices which should excuse him from being mindful of his words. Swaying back and forth in sync with each sentence as if his statements seemed to be too powerful for his small frame to support such truths. Davion imposes his presence. "Stop all that lying! Sarge, I thought honor was the corner stone of your character."

Sarge turns around with an angry grin. "How dare someone interrupt the Sarge with talks of dishonor!"

Catfish speaks next. "Shut the fuck up you dumb ass soldier. It's nephew."

Sarge's angry grin turns to a scowl and the rhythmic wavering ceases. "You shut the fuck up! I know who the fuck it is. You stupid ass stankin' mutherfucka."

"Nigga, fuck you with a big dick." Catfish answers

back.

Davion intervenes. "Gentleman this is an unnecessary cause for an argument."

Moses interjects. "Word. I didn't come over here to hear y'all argue about who the stankinest or who the dumbest.

Baghdad buts in. "Nephew, who is this lil nigga talking shit."

Moses tenses up. "What the fuck did you say?"

"Nephew, you need to holla at you boy before his ass get chopped down." Sarge commands.

Moses' brow curls as he takes an aggressive step towards Sarge. Davion puts his hand up and gives him a glance and then focuses his stare at Sarge who immediately shuts down. "This is my nephew." Davion says with a smile.

"Nephew?!" Moses says with disdain. "Cut that bullshit out. You ain't that much older than me."

The crowd laughs, and the tension has dissipated. Davion receives a text from Jabari that the car is at his house. Davion tells Moses to hang out with Sarge and crew until he comes back. Moses sits there with them on the corner, under god's robe as children with the knowledge of men but not the wisdom, and he saw the potential of letting himself become 'nephew'.

Davion walks back home to see the broken

glass on his porch and Jabari in the driveway with the rental. "What is all this?"

"I don't know. It was like that when we got here." Jabari responds.

"Got damn Nadia." Davion says in disgust. "I don't have time for this right now. What happened with Doris?"

Jabari laughing. "It's all good. That crazy bitch smoked up almost all the crack we gave her before we got back and threw up all over Jeff's coat. You should have saw his face."

Davion not amused. "What do you mean the crack you GAVE her?"

Jabari stutters. "Noo. We let her get it on credit like you said."

Davion baffled. "Why the fuck...Never mind. I need to make some pickups and you need to handle the Doris situation ASAP."

Jabari confidently responds. "Don't worry we already put the fear of Jesus in her if she didn't have the money."

"I don't care about how, just go get the money." He gets in the car and rolls down the window. "And no pussy payments for fucks sake." Davion leaves Jabari to walk to his next destination in frustration.

After making a few pickups, Davion receives a frantic call from Jabari. "They got Moses. That crackhead bitch is dead, and bitches is kidnapping bitches at your house."

Davion noticeably surprised, interrupts.   "Slow down. Who got Moses? What the fuck happened? Where are you now?"

Jabari follows his instructions. "I'm at your crib."

Davion cuts him off before he finishes. "Say less. I'm on my way."

Davion pulls over to think, realizing that his plans are falling apart. He knows the 3Js aren't capable of running an operation and he still needs to leave town today. Then he considers his last pickup and how capable Levar is at keeping a low profile and making decent business decisions. He decides that letting Levar run things while he's gone until he can find a better candidate is the best option. He calls Levar to let him know.

"What up doe." Levar answers in a gravelly voice.

"Rise and shine princess. I need to holler at you about something when I get there." Davion replies.

Levar's voice becomes alert and remotely panicked. "You on your way now!?" He can be heard shuffling around over the phone.   "No problem I got the money but some of it is jewelry."

Davion not too happy about the jewelry but still desperate. "No worries, but I still need to holler at you about something else."

Levar relieved by the response. "Cool. I'll be posted

at the crib until you get here."

"Alright but I have to make a stop first." Davion hangs up the phone and then proceeds to meet with Jabari and get the details about what happened.

Davion pulls up to the house where Jabari is pacing and talking to himself smoking a black and mild cigar. Davion approaches and Jabari wastes no time in telling him what happened.

"This shit is crazy. First me and Joe go to get the money from crackhead Doris but we thought she wasn't home so we broke in to take what we could. We don't find no money just a bunch of U of M papers and college applications and shit. And then Joe sees her body on the floor just dead as hell. We get up out of there and then head to the gas station. That shit was even crazier than Doris's house. Twelve was at the gas station and Sarge told us that Moses went crazy after smoking a laced blunt and start killing everybody. Then the nigga tripped and fell in the street and got hit by a bus."

"What. The. Fuck." The only words Davion can muster.

Jabari continues. "Then me and Jeff come to tell you what happened and we see some bitches dragging Doris' daughter into a car in front of your house, but they pulled off before we called you. And that's pretty much it."

Davion beyond exasperated. "Let me get this straight. Doris is dead, Moses got hit by a bus, and crazy ass Nadia and her girls kidnapped Doris' college bound daughter."

Jabari nods. "Yup. That sounds about right."

"Just go back to the spot and post up till I call you. I have about one more stop to make." Davion gets back in the car cuts on the radio and contemplates his order from coney island before going to Levar's.

Davion, reenergized with food, arrives at Levar's house. When he is about to ring the doorbell, he notices the door is not locked and walks in and yells. "A Var! You know your door is open! Where you at?" He puts his hand on his gun as he enters the house. He sees Levar's body. "Aw shit! You gotta be kidding me." He looks and listens and concludes that no one else is still there. He gathers his thoughts and chooses to look for the money hoping that his murder was personal since the house was not ransacked. He ransacks the apartment looking for the money and finds nothing except the earring that Nadia was wearing when she left his house that morning. "Who the fuck is this bitch, and why is she everywhere ruining my life!" He exclaims while picking up the earring, hating its recognition. Furious and at wits end, he calls Jabari.

"Sup boss." Jabari answers casually.

"I need y'all to tool up and wait at my house." Davion says authoritatively.

"Fasho, what's the problem? We got you." Jabari states vigorously.

"They about to do a drive by on the crib. I need y'all to set up and be ready, so that when they show up y'all can execute them mutherfuckas."

"Don't worry about nothing. We got this shit handled." Jabari assures Davion with murderous intent.

"Good. I'm on my way. I'll get there when I get there." Davion ends the call and sends a couple dirty messages to N'vaeh's phone knowing that Nadia would see them.

Davion finally arrives back at home and sees the aftermath of the shootout with the 3Js and Nadia's crew. He notices Robin's car and doesn't see Nadia until he looks toward the corner and sees her running away. He follows and watches Nadia holding Sarge and N'vaeh at gunpoint.

Nadia intent on killing N'vaeh. "Move unc this don't have nothing to do with you. This puppy needs to be put down."

Sarge pleads. "You are too young to put yourself in this situation. Please don't." He covers N'vaeh's body with his.

Davion approaches an unaware Nadia as she squeezes the trigger and shoots her in the back of the head in unison splattering blood on Sarge as he protects N'vaeh. "Nooo!" Sarge exclaims clutching N'vaeh's motionless body as Nadia's lifeless corpse drops to her knees.

Sarge looks up in anguish and relief due to being shot by Nadia, realizing that N'vaeh was only pretending to be hurt and the blood pooling was his own. He sees that Davion has saved them. "Thanks Nephew." He groans.

"Don't thank me." Davion reflects on his warning to Sarge and the fact that he is N'vaeh's last bit of family. "Forgive me." Then shoots him. He lowers his gun then looks at N'vaeh with consoling eyes. "It's over now, you can go home."

N'vaeh still stunned from the situation. "I don't think I can." Then she remembers the money that Nadia had stashed and retrieves the bag from her shirt. "Can you help me?" She offers the bag to Davion.

Davion takes the bag, removes a watch from the jewelry, half the money and hands it back to N'vaeh. He bends down and looks her in the eyes with his finger on his lips. "Can you keep a secret Ms. Wolverine?"

N'vaeh looks at him, reflects on her day, how he knows about school and deduces he knows about her mother. She smiles a hurtful smile. "Only if you can."

"You already know that I do...little sis." He says with a wink and a smile.

They both part ways happy that this chapter is over but keeping in mind that the day is only getting started.

AFTERWORD: A MESSAGE FROM THE NARRATOR

If you've made it this far, then let's start from the beginning one more time. Can you decipher the message below?

1IIj 61Xc 1IIb 52Ii 2Vb 2XIh 7XIIIb 8Ic 18IXe.
49IIIa 5IVe 12IVg 57XXg 24Ij 71XVf 88IIIf 75IIe.